# You're Safe Now, Waterdog

Richard Edwards

*Illustrated by*
Sophy Williams

VIKING

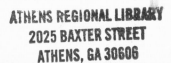

VIKING
Published by the Penguin Group

Penguin Books USA Inc., 375 Hudson Street, New York, New York 10014, U.S.A.
Penguin Books Ltd, 27 Wrights Lane, London W8 5TZ, England
Penguin Books Australia Ltd, Ringwood, Victoria, Australia
Penguin Books Canada Ltd, 10 Alcorn Avenue, Toronto, Ontario, Canada M4V 3B2
Penguin Books (N.Z.) Ltd, 182-190 Wairu Road, Auckland 10, New Zealand
Penguin Books Ltd, Registered Offices: Harmondsworth, Middlesex, England

First published in Great Britain in 1996 by Orion Children's Books,
a division of the Orion Publishing Group Ltd
First published in the United States of America in 1997 by Viking,
a division of Penguin Books USA Inc.

10 9 8 7 6 5 4 3 2 1     1 2 3 4 5 6 7 8 9 10
1 3 5 7 9 10 8 6 4 2

Text copyright © Richard Edwards, 1996
Illustrations copyright © Sophy Williams, 1996
All rights reserved.
Library of Congress Catalog Card Number: 96-60979
ISBN 0-670-87385-3
Printed in Italy
Set in Baskerville
Designed by Dalia Hartman

Watt the dog and Matt were always together.

They played together.

They went shopping together.

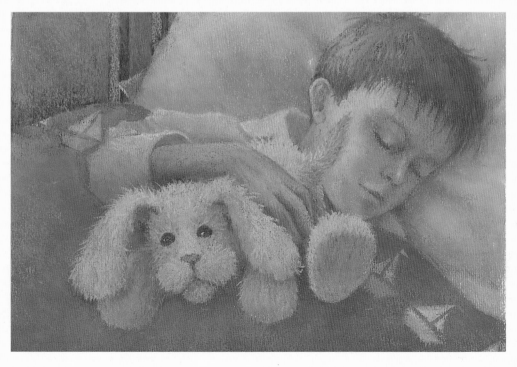

They curled up in the same bed together.

Matt took Watt everywhere…

…exploring,

climbing,

even to school.

But as Matt grew up he began to forget about Watt the dog.

So sometimes Watt stayed at home when Matt went out on his bicycle,

or sat cramped in a dusty corner when Matt got into bed.

One day after Matt had been out playing with his friends, Watt was left behind on the river bank, and no one came back to look for him.

Watt lay all alone beside the river. Owls hooted in the treetops, and a fox sniffed at Watt before slinking away into the darkness.

Then it began to rain.

Rain fell on the woods and fields. Rain
filled the ditches and poured into the river
until the water swirled round Watt, lifting
him up and carrying him away.

Spinning and ducking, Watt the waterdog drifted downstream, past herds of staring cows, past farms and fishermen, through villages, under bridges.

At first he floated well, but the longer his journey lasted the colder and soggier he got, until only his head was left bobbing above the surface.

Hattie was splashing about
by the river trying to scoop up
leaves when Watt drifted past.

She reached out with her net but
missed. She reached again and missed
again, but the third time she stretched
just far enough to lift Watt out of the
water and carry him proudly home.
  "Look. A waterdog!"

Watt lay in front of a warm fire, gently steaming. When he was dry he sat at the table while Hattie ate her supper.

At bedtime Hattie carried Watt to her room and tucked him into a shoebox on her bedside table.

But when the light was out and the door was closed, she lifted him out of the box.

"You're safe now, waterdog," she whispered.

And she hugged him tight and fell asleep with Watt the Waterdog cuddled in her arms.